30 Flash Horror Stories

By

Dawn Colclasure

Published in the United States of America
First eBook Edition: October 16, 2023

Acknowledgments

Many thanks to my family for their neverending patience and support.

Thank you also to Maria Elena Vogt and Ruth Burroughs for suggesting resources.

Dedication

For my nephew, Aaron, with love

Table of Contents

Author's Notes

When I gave myself the task of putting together a collection of 30 horror flash fiction stories in less than a month (because that's how much I love myself), at first I thought I couldn't do it. I even tried to get out of it, hoping I could change the cover I already had for this book to read "10" instead of "30." Because ten was totally doable! But I wasn't able to do that, so I was stuck with thirty.

Thirty!

I actually threw a fit. I can't write thirty flash fiction stories in less than a month! No way! Not with everything else I already have going on!

After I had that little outburst, I sat down to start writing it.

It helped that I decided to make these storis no more than 500 words each. With flash fiction, you have some flexibility. You can write drabbles, which are 100-word stories (I have written many), or flash, which is anywhere between 100-1000 word stories. (Anything less than 100 words are called micro fiction stories.) And while this word limit was helpful in giving me the confidence to be able to write the stories, it did present a challenge in its own right. I ended up having to cut a lot of words to get to 500! Some stories, though, ended up being less than 500 words.

And because these stories were so short, I wrote MANY of them on my smartphone.

I surprised myself with actually getting closer and closer to that number of thirty stories. I managed to get ideas for stories in a variety of ways.

One of the stories, "A Good Deed," had been in my head for years.

The idea for "Spaghetti Face" came to me after I created a face out of spaghetti at dinner one night.

I got the idea for "What We Do in the Dark" after I noticed that, because of my frequent headaches, we often leave the lights off in the house anytime I'm dealing with them.

"Finding a Body" came to me one day after I was driving past a park and noticed a local crisis response unit there along with the police.

"The Scary Costume" is based on a poem I'd written that has the same story.

I used to work as a DSP supporting individuals with Intellectual/ Developmental Disabilities (I/DD) and while I loved that job, some days were a big challenge and those days would exhaust us and really test our patience. I got the idea for "A Bunch of Whiners" based on one particular coworker who I had a difficult time working with on top of the challenges associated with the job, and while the DSP in this story acts out, that never happened with this coworker. But I kept wondering, What would happen if he lost it? While I know what happens in the story would not happen in real life, for the purpose of fiction, I decided to add some plot twists.

"Departure Time" was inspired by an article I read in the newspaper.

"Killer Toes" is the result of a typo that came up on an iPad I used for my work as a DSP. (Don't ask!) I saw that and thought, That could be a story title!

The idea for "Teacher Problems" came to me after my youngest said he didn't want to attend Open House at his school.

Some of the stories, such as "Routines" and "Monday Coffee, are revisions of other drabbles or flash stories that never made the cut anywhere I submitted them to.

And other stories – such as "Gore Galore" and "No Rest for the Wicked" – came to me as titles. I just took it from there.

Aside from all that, sometimes, I just had ideas for stories pop into my head, as was the case for "The Sign" and "Her Last Halloween." An idea wasn't enough to get me writing the story, though. I had to think about it! I had to work with that idea and figure out how to turn it into a story. Thankfully, I did manage to figure it out and get those stories written.

Some days, I wrote several stories, and others I only managed to write one or two stories. Then there was the odd day I wasn't able to write any stories at all! (The horror!) But I did keep up with writing the stories. Every so often. I would count how many stories I had so far and plan out how many more to write.

When I started writing these stories, my intention was to make it a collection of horror stories (since horror and paranormal stories are my thing right now). But as I continued writing, some of the story ideas tied into Halloween and I also ended up writing stories that had elements of Halloween in them. I guess, since I'm writing these stories during October, that was bound to happen. (Halloween is my favorite holiday, so maybe that influenced the stories too.)

And while my focus with all this story-writing was to write 500-word stories, sometimes the stories I wrote were longer. Many were 1000 words. I decided to put THOSE stories into a different collection of flash fiction stories, which I plan to write at leisure!

Writing this story collection has been a fun challenge for me. It reminded me of the time I challenged myself to write a short story every week for one year – except this time, my stories were shorter, and I had to write them in one day instead of one week.

Writing flash fiction can be a fun writing exercise for some, but a challenge for others. It can especially be a challenge for the kind of writers who are purists for writing fiction, such as following the "rules" of fiction writing and writing the stories in the same way as writing a normal short story. But with flash fiction, some elements of fiction writing, such as description and characterization, must be sacrificed in order to meet word count limits. In some cases, I do throw in bits and pieces of character description, but for the most part, I leave what the characters look like up to the readers' imagination.

Another thing I leave to the readers' imagination are endings. Some stories have open endings, where the reader can decide what happens next.

If you have always wanted to write a story or would like to give flash fiction a try, then I hope the information shared here will give you a good idea on where to start. Ideas for stories are everywhere, and sometimes we have to twist thigs around a bit in order to make a story "work" or fit into the genre we are writing for, such as horror, fantasy or science fiction. It's also a good idea to decide how long you want your flash fiction story to be. Remember, you can write a drabble, which is 50 or 100 words, or you can write a story of up to 1000 words. It is entirely your choice. Once you get better at writing flash fiction, you can experiment with different word counts and genres.

But flash writing is not limited to just fiction. There is also flash nonfiction. These are "mini essays" or mini stories of something that happened in real life.

You just may find that writing flash fiction can be addictive! I'm used to writing longer things, but being able to write a story in less than an hour is a very satisfying feeling. So satisfying that I tend to write many more!

The beauty of writing flash fiction is that it can be done really quickly. With just 50 or 100 words, you have written a story! So give it a try, if you feel so inclined. If you're not sure about what to write or how to write flash, check out my list of writing books included at the back of this book. It includes some titles that can help you with the writing of flash fiction.

I hope some of these stories will inspire you with your own story ideas. You can also get ideas for things to write from your ow life – your experiences, your dreams and observations. A lot of the stories I write come from my own personal experiences and from dreams.

The thing I love about writing flash fiction is that it forces a writer to be careful with their word choice. When writing flash fiction, you only get so many words to write. In that limited space where you must deliver a story with dialogue, characterization, description, etc., you must also write tight. Choose your words carefully. Write "many" instead of "a lot." Use the word "teased" instead of "made fun of." Also, when you have to cut words in order to meet the word count limit, keep the most important stuff. If you must show that a character spoke with a "deep voice," then find another word somewhere else to delete.

What can really help you in learning how to write flash fiction, though, is to read flash fiction. And lots of it! Look at how other writers tell their stories in 50, 100 or even 1000 words. Notice the words they choose and how they show the action happening.

If books are your thing for learning, then here are some titles that can help you get started:

- *The World in a Flash: How to Write Flash-Fiction* by Calum Kerr
- *Writing Flash Fiction: How to Write Very Short Stories and Get Them Published* by Carly Berg
- *FLASH!: Writing the Very Short Story* by John Dufresne
- *The Rose Metal Press Field Guide to Writing Flash Fiction: Tips from Editors, Teachers, and Writers in the Field* by Tara L. Masih.

My friend and fellow author, Ruth Burroughs, knows flash fiction writing well. She is an award-winning writer of flash fiction and author of a book of flash fiction stories (which I really enjoyed reading!) called *Michelangelo 2000 and other microstories: a collection of short science fiction stories*[1]

---

1. https://www.amazon.com/Michelangelo-2000-other-microstories-collection-ebook/dp/

B095HXDZ5N/?_encoding=UTF8&pd_rd_w=WVtdZ&content-id=amzn1.sym.579192ca-1482-4409-

Here are some articles Ruth recommends to writers interested in writing flash fiction:

"A Crash Course in Flash Fiction: An Essential Reading List of Very Short Stories"[2] by Laura I. Miller (via LitHub)

"10 Hands-On Tips For Writing Flash Fiction"[3] by Maria Haskins (via the Science Fiction & Fantasy Writers Association)

"Top 24 Websites for Flash Fiction"[4] (via Bookfox)

No matter how new or experienced of a writer you may be, writing flash fiction can be an entertaining diversion as well as a challenge in writing with concision. Flash fiction writing takes some practice to get it right, but if you give it a try and have patience, it just might be one kind of writing you will eventually excel at.

Enjoy the stories!

abe7-9e14f17ac827&pf_rd_p=579192ca-1482-4409-abe7-9e14f17ac827&pf_rd_r=131-7116304-2623756&pd_rd_wg=kRZCd&pd_rd_r=9d67029c-afe1-45eb-bf9h-ed9538364d4e&ref_=aufs_ap_sc_dsk&fbclid=IwAR332kddsrOKyu-bkGqDZWVBKTOSKejRCSbiotuQ4BrN9w9LXft3KnZ0E-I

2.   https://lithub.com/a-crash-course-in-flash-fiction/?fbclid=IwAR3xkfRx2shmgsnscRvuPrOhd7gSq0Mbhg9BwmCOS9zen4dHTXOm4RX7hUI

3.   https://www.sfwa.org/2022/03/15/10-tips-flash-fiction/?fbclid=IwAR1lkK_XTMXBt4BIfTQKcfOshOog2JJIOXxXnPHPpJ74BJrL441-TCRUF6U

4.   https://thejohnfox.com/2021/08/top-24-websites-for-flash-fiction/?fbclid=IwAR3wVqkiwx1Efsv1vo3UvcgMO84kesfDkVrgQwiIlEF8FPUwIWCN7GsZ7Us

—Dawn Colclasure
Eugne, Oregon
October 2023

A Departing Gift

"You son of a bitch, you killed my baby!"

The woman continued pounding on the chest of the cuffed man, who the boy knew to be her boyfriend.

He wished he could hit the man, too. After all, he had just sat on him and killed him. Even though the boy knew he hadn't meant to kill him.

Still, rage seethed through him. "Tomorrow is Christmas, and I won't be able to open my presents!" he screamed at the man.

The man gave no indication that he could hear him. He only stood there, helpless to fight off the girlfriend attacking him.

The police seemed to focus on the body lying on the floor instead of what was happening to their prisoner. Which was fine with him.

The boy looked down at his body. The paramedics were still using the portable automated external defibrillator to try to shock the boy to life, without success.

The ghostly figure of the boy looked to the Christmas tree, where all of his presents were never going to be opened. A new surge of raise flooded through him. His Christmas had been stolen from him!

He walked over to stand near the boyfriend, who the cops were now finally trying to pry the sobbing woman away from as she attempted to strangle him. He focused his rage on him, sending it out to him in one burst.

The man turned his head and looked directly where the boy stood. At first, he blinked rapidly, not sure of what he was seeing. Then his expression turned to horror.

"No!" he gasped.

The boy focused his hate, sending it directly to the man's heart.

"Merry Christmas," he said.

The man's heart exploded and his body fell to the floor.

A Good Deed

After Gerald awoke, one thing was on his mind: He must do a good deed today. He tried to do a good deed every day. Good deeds made him feel happy.

It was nice to feel happy.

He went about his morning routines – showering, getting dressed, breakfast and brushing his teeth – then, just as he usually did at 11AM every day, he set out for his walk in the neighborhood.

There had to be a good deed waiting for him somewhere.

He smiled at the people he encountered on the sidewalk and made sure he waited until the light was green on the stoplight before crossing the street. He enjoyed the cool autumn breeze blowing through his hair and took time to appreciate assorted Halloween decorations at different houses.

Then he found it. His good deed.

Gasping with delight, he eagerly picked up the thing he found in the bushes in the park. Funny it was in there. He didn't know how it got there; someone must have dropped it. No matter; he had to return it to the owner. That would be his good deed for the day.

But who was the owner?

He looked around but couldn't see anyone who appeared to be looking for a lost item.

Maybe he should walk around a bit in the park to find them. He smiled. Yes, maybe they were busy looking somewhere else. They had no idea where their lost thing was, but he did! He had found it! He had to get it back to them.

He clutched it against himself as he walked, keeping an eye out for anyone looking for something.

Then the voice spoke. "Gerald, what are you doing?"

"A good deed," Gerald replied in his mind.

"But how will you find who that belongs to? What if they're gone?"

Gerald hunched his shoulders in determination. "I will find them," he whispered in response.

Then he did: There was a man on his knees, looking under a park bench for something. He was probably looking for the thing Gerald had!

Gerald hurried over to him. "Hey, mister!" he said, standing behind the man's crouched figure.

The man barely glanced back at him. "What do you want?"

"I found it," Gerald said, holding the item out.

The man jumped to his feet, looking at Gerald expectantly. But when he saw the item, his look turned to horror and he recoiled. "That's not mine," he said.

"But it is!" Gerald insisted. "You were looking for it."

The man shook his head. "No. Not that."

"Just take it! It's yours!" Gerald encouraged, holding the item out to the man.

The man tried to run but Gerald pushed the item towards him. In the scuffle, the bloody knife's blade went into the man's stomach.

The man cried out and fell to his knees.

Gerald smiled. "There. You have it back now. I've done my good deed."

He turned to walk away, oblivious of the people running to the man's aid.

A Mother Scorned

"Let me in," Owen demanded, icily staring Tabitha down.

Tabitha sniffed, staring right back at him. "Over my dead body."

Owen grinned. "That can be arranged."

She hardened her gaze, refusing to let him see how much that unnerved her. "Like you did with the other ones?"

His grin disappeared. "You shut up about that! You think you can stop me from having claim to my own children? They're still mine!"

Tabitha scowled. "Sperm doesn't make you their father," she icily shot back. "You only call them your children when it's convenient for you. Now get out of here, before I call the cops."

Owen chuckled. "Go ahead and call them," he said. "Call the cops!" He stepped towards her. "And we'll see whose side they're on. That badge gives me more than just a job, you know."

Tabitha gulped but she did everything to make sure he didn't see her fear. "I still have custody," she reminded. "I don't care how crooked your friends are. My name is on that legal document saying they are mine. You will never take them from me!"

"Mommy?"

Tabitha gulped, swinging her head around to see her 9-year-old daughter standing behind her, clutching her brown teddy bear.

Before she could say anything to calm her daughter, she looked back just to see Owen say to her, "We'll see about that."

She opened her mouth to speak but he stormed off her front porch.

She forced the sobs down as she watched him leave. She knew he'd be back, just like he came back so many nights before, just to terrorize her.

She slammed the door shut and locked it. Then she turned to kneel down to hug her daughter close to her as she cried.

#

That evening, Tabitha made sure everything was in place. The alarm was set, the shotgun was loaded and her phone was fully charged. As her children slept, she started to ask herself if she was really willing to go as far as killing Owen to protect them.

It didn't take much thinking to decide she would.

She had drifted off when he did show up that night. Sherman's barking woke her up.

Gripping the shotgun, she looked out the window to see Owen striding up the walkway. He, too, had a gun, only his was smaller.

She got to the door before him and swung it open. Owen stopped as she pointed the gun at him.

"You gonna shoot me?" he asked. He laughed. "Go right ahead!"

She pulled the trigger but it caught.

Owen laughed, holding up his pistol. "Goodbye!" he roared, walking towards her.

A ghostly figured swooped in front of Owen, knocking him off his feet. It hovered over Owen and an audible sound of his neck breaking resounded in Tabitha's ears.

The ghostly figure disappeared.

Lowering the gun to the floor, she stepped over him to check for a pulse. There was none.

"That works too," she said, looking up. She smiled. "Thank you."

An Urban Legend

"We need to get out of here before dark," Analise reminded her boyfriend, as he drove through the town.

He scoffed. "Right now, the time of day is the least of my worries." He scanned the area ahead. "We need a gas station more than anything else."

"But you know what happens to people wandering through this town at night, Steven!"

He shook his head. "Don't worry, we'll be gone by then. I hope."

Analise looked to the fuel gauge and noted that the needle was very close to the "E." She looked out the windshield as Steven continued to drive through the desert town, trying to help him find a gas station. "Why didn't you get on the freeway before you got low on gas?"

"Because we came to check this place out, and I'll be damned if we leave before we get to check this place out."

She frowned. "Ok. Let's park somewhere and check it out on foot." She looked at him. "Maybe we'll have better luck finding a gas station."

After a bit of quiet driving, he replied. "Okay."

He decided to park the car in the parking lot of a local park. Once the car was off, Analise removed her seatbelt and climbed out. She stretched and sighed. "Guess we could use some time to stretch our legs, anyway."

"I agree," Steven said, walking around the car to join her. "Let's go be tourists."

Chuckling, she followed him.

They spent hours checking out the supposed "ghost town" they'd heard so much about, without finding a gas station.

As the sky darkened, Analise looked at Steven with worry. "We should go now. Remember what they said about this place?"

Steven laughed. "It's just an urban legend. No way would a huge skull really chase people through town after dark."

Analise wanted to believe him, but as the sky grew darker, she got a bad feeling.

A feeling which was confirmed when they came upon a building with a brilliant white light shining at the side. They stopped walking and stared in bewilderment.

They stood and watched as the light grew brighter. A large white skull floated into view, facing them. They froze with terror, wondering if their eyes were deceiving them.

"Then what's that?" she asked, pointing.

Her blood chilled as the large white floating skull flew towards them, loudly chomping its teeth.

"Run!" Analise screamed.

They turned and raced along the dirt road. Analise whimpered as she heard the crunching sounds of her boyfriend being eaten by the skull behind her, his blood hitting the back of her body as she ran.

She screamed as the giant teeth came down on her, crumbling her body into bits.

Bucket List

"I just added 'climb Mt. Everest' to my bucket list," a father announced to his son one day.

His 10-year-old looked up at him. "What's a bucket list?"

"A bucket list is a list of things you want to do before you die," his father explained.

"Oh." He thought about this then looked up at his dad again. "When will you do them?"

His father shrugged. "Oh, later on in life. After you're older."

"But why wait, Dad? You don't know how much time you've got left."

His father thought about this then smiled. "You know, son, you're right! Maybe I should start doing those things right now. I'll start packing for my trip."

"What trip?" the boy asked, following his dad into the bedroom.

"My trip to Australia, of course!" his father answered. "It's the first thing on my list."

The boy's eyes brightened and he smiled. "Cool! Can I come?"

"Sorry, son. This is a solo vacation." His father made a call on his cell phone as he left the room.

The boy followed his father out of the room. He waited until his father finished his call then tugged on his arm. "But who's going to take care of me while you're gone?"

"Don't worry," his father assured. "Your uncle Charlie will be here while I'm away. In fact, he's on his way here right now!"

Ten minutes later, there was a knock at the front door. His father opened the door to a man on the doorstep. A man the boy recognized as his uncle. "Come in!" he cheered, grabbing Uncle Charlie's hand for a handshake as he stepped into the house. "Thanks so much for doing this on short notice."

"My pleasure," Uncle Charlie replied, smiling. "Go off and have fun! Beasley and I will have a great time together!"

Beasley recoiled as his uncle drew closer, hungrily staring at the child's neck. "Uh, Dad. There's something you should know about Uncle Charlie," he said.

But his father was already out the door carrying his suitcase, just as Uncle Charlie's fangs sank into his neck.

Bunch of Whiners

Anton sighed as he parked his car at work. Another day in paradise, he dryly thought. Well, hopefully, one of the other jobs he applied for will come through soon.

He grabbed his backpack then got out of the car. He checked that he had his phone in his pants pocket then locked the car. He took his time walking into work, wishing he was anywhere else but here.

After clocking in, he entered the main building. Since he was the first one on shift, he had to hand out the morning medications to the three individuals at the facility. Once that was done, he made breakfast then helped his charges to the table so they could eat. While they ate, he tore the sheets and blankets off of the beds then carried the bedding to the washroom. He threw them into the washing machine and started it up.

After breakfast, he bathed the individuals and got them into clean clothes.

When the three of them were sitting in the living room watching TV, Anton started to wonder if his co-staff was ever going to show up. It was almost ten.

His phone vibrated. He removed it from his pocket and read the text from his manager: "Bella called off. You're on your own today."

"Shit!" he exclaimed, slapping his forehead. Realizing he had just used profanity in front of the individuals, he cocked his head in their direction to see if it had affected them. Two of them gave him a worried look before they continued watching TV, while the third hummed as he conducted an imaginary orchestra with his hands.

Anton got busy cleaning the kitchen. He finished cleaning the bedrooms and vacuumed the living room carpet.

One of the individuals appeared in the bathroom doorway while Anton was busy cleaning it. "I want to go shopping," he said. "Today is my day to shop."

Anton shook his head. "It will have to wait for tomorrow."

"But I'm supposed to go today!" he complained.

"We can't go because I'm the only one here," Anton explained, trying to restrain himself from shouting. "We can go for a drive."

"A drive isn't shopping," the individual grumbled.

After their lunch and medications, Anton loaded them into the van for a drive.

"I want ice cream!" one individual complained, after they had set off.

"I want to go shopping!" another whined.

Anton banged his hand on the steering wheel. "Will you guys knock it off!" he yelled. "We're on a drive!" Then he grumbled, "Geez, you're all a bunch of whiners!"

They remained silent after that.

Once returning to the facility, Anton prepared dinner. While he poured tater tots onto a cookie sheet, he heard footsteps behind him.

He placed the bag of frozen tots down and turned.

He barely caught sight of something resembling a baseball bat flying in the air before it hit him square in the face. He flew backwards, landing against the other individual, who twisted his neck.

Doing the Impossible

"I can't do it!" Theo whined, throwing the book down onto the floor.

His friend just stared at him.

Scowling, Theo tore the robe off. "Let's just forget it, okay? This was a dumb idea."

His friend frowned. "No, it's not. You said you wanted to know what a human brain looks like. Well, this is the best way to see what it looks like." He looked around to make sure there was nobody in the garage who might have overheard them. "Well, a real one, anyway. Not something on the screen like in a video."

Theo sighed. "But I've never cut open a head before." He looked down at the corpse. "It's impossible."

His friend sighed. "Fine! I'll do it!"

He shoved Theo out of the way. As he took the scalpel and began cutting, Theo watched. His friend must have done this before, because he didn't even need to look at the book for directions.

Eventually, his friend pulled the brain out of the skull and held it up for Theo to examine. "See? Not so impossible. Here is a brain!"

"Hey!"

The teens froze, the realization that they were caught by a parent written across their faces.

But Theo screamed and his friend turned around. He got a look at what was standing behind him and also screamed.

The corpse they had just removed the brain from stood there, scowling. It stood perhaps a foot taller than the two of them. "You put that back!" it demanded.

The brain was thrown into the corpse's hands and the boys screamed as they ran out of the garage.

Exploding Rage

She looked straight at her donnas he sat across from her at the table. "Eat."

The boy seemed to take it as a challenge because he hardened his gaze. "No."

She pushed the plate containing tied chicken leg and mashed potatoes closer to him. "We had a deal. You could have the cookies before dinner as long as you ate your dinner. And you promised you would eat it. You promised!"

Her 9-year-old smiled at her. "You promised I could get that you at the store, but I didn't!"

She looked at him with confusion. "What?"

"When we went to the store today," her son answered. "You promised I could get a ray gun if I was good. I was good, but you didn't let me get it!"

Her look of anger returned. "I didn't have enough money."

"You never have enough money to buy me things, but you always have enough money to buy your stupid beer!"

"That doesn't matter!" she yelled. "Now eat your damn food, or you can how to bed without dinner!"

"I'm not hungry," he sneered.

"Then you don't get dinner!" She yelled, standing to throw the plate of food at the wall.

The plate shattered against the wall, and as the food flew everywhere, a large shard from the glass plate flew backwards and hit the mother in the middle of her forehead, planting itself within her brain.

Her lifeless body fell back on the floor.

Finding a Body

One thing my best friend Drew and I shared was a curiosity for dead bodies. Real ones. Anytime Drew and I were out and there was a police cruiser parked somewhere, he'd say, "I bet they found a body."

One time, he was right.

It was at a neighborhood park. Yellow tape cleared off the area and there were cops, detectives and other people spread out.

We hid in the nearby bushes, so we got a good view of it: A lady with long black hair. Her body was blue and bloated. They must have found her in the lake.

A dead body! I'd never seen a real one before. "The skin is mushy," I said.

"Look how pieces of the arm are missing," Drew said, pointing. "Like fish ate it."

"Hey! You kids!"

We turned to see a police officer towering over us.

"Get out of here!" he barked.

We jumped to our feet and ran away.

"That was so cool!" Drew enthused, as we walked down the street.

"I know, right!" I answered, grinning. "It looked even better than in the movies."

"We're still on for tonight, right?" Drew asked.

I grinned. "Of course! I've got my Batman costume. You have the Robin costume?"

Drew stopped. "I was going to be Batman."

I stopped a couple of steps ahead of him, looking back. "What? No. I was going to be Batman."

"You were Batman last year," Drew reminded, folding his arms over his chest. "It's my turn."

"Hey, kids."

We turned to look at a guy wearing torn bloody clothes and dirty hair grinning at us with stained teeth. "You wanna see some bodies?"

Drew and I exchanged excited looks.

"Hell yes!" Drew answered.

He waved us on to follow and we did. We went to what must have been his house, which had all these cool Halloween decorations out front. "It must be a haunt attraction," Drew whispered to me. We went in.

Inside the house, there was a musty smell, but we still followed the guy to a room. He opened the door and we went in.

We looked around the room as we entered. The walls were covered with blood and there were three human bodies scattered on the floor.

"Cool!" I cried, looking at the butchered bodies. One of them, a man, was without a head. There were two teen girls with throats slit and cuts all over them.

Drew, however, was not impressed. "Oh, come on," he whined, as though he was an expert. "These are obviously fake bodies."

"They're still cool Halloween decorations, though," I pointed out.

"They're not decorations," the stranger said, picking up a large machete with blood on it. "They're real."

He turned to smile at us. "And now you get to join them."

We screamed and ran out of the room then out of the house. After we got to my house, Drew and I decided that we never wanted to see anymore real dead bodies ever again.

Ghosts

Slam!

"Did you hear that?" Melody gasped, standing stone still.

Her twin sister looked at her with wide eyes and nodded. "Of course I heard it."

Melody licked her lips. "Stephanie, I told you, we have ghosts!"

The look of fear disappeared from Stephanie's face and, being the sensible one, she gently squeezed her sister's hand. "That's impossible. Ghosts aren't real."

Melody was having none of it. In her entire sixteen years, she had come across many ghost stories, especially the true kind. She placed her hands on her hip. "Of course they're real! How do you explain the doors opening and closing all the time? The curtains opening by themselves? The piano playing by itself?"

Stephanie frowned. "I'm sure there is a logical explanation for it all."

When Melody didn't relax at this suggestion, Stephanie rubbed her arm. "Come on. Mom and Dad will be home soon. Let's make the house look really nice for them, okay?" She smiled. "It will be a nice surprise."

Melody grinned. "I hope they brought us presents back from Europe!"

Stephanie nodded. "Me, too! And now that we're not sick anymore, maybe they will be able to take us with them when they have to leave again."

As the sisters walked through the living room, Melody grew lost in thought. Then she looked at Stephanie and said, "That sickness was awful! I never thought we'd make it!"

"Me, too," Stephanie agreed. "And it lasted for so long! I guess the new medicine the doctor tried giving us finally did the trick."

They continued chatting as they moved across the room, once again not noticing how easily the two of them walked right through the walls.

Gore Galore

Bruce opened the door and smiled at the sight of his buddy, Toby, standing on his porch.

Toby entered the apartment and Bruce closed the door. He turned to see his friend pumping his fists in the air.

"Dude!" Toby cried. "Watching horror movies on Halloween night is killer!"

Bruce nodded then held up a finger. "And! We get all the candy to ourselves!"

"Right on!" Toby cheered.

The two ran into the living room and plopped themselves down on the couch. A bowl of assorted candy bars was on the coffee table, along with bags of chips, assorted cans of soda and a large bowl of popcorn.

"I can't believe your mom's okay with this," Toby said, shaking his head as Bruce put on a horror movie.

"Dude, I grew up on this stuff!" Bruce replied, sitting next to his friend on the couch.

They watched a couple of horror movies, relishing in the gory scenes and commenting on creative murder scenes.

Toby grabbed a movie from the stack of DVDs on the shelf. "*Gore Galore*?" he read.

Bruce shrugged. "Found it at a yard sale."

"Perfect!" Toby cheered. He removed the disc from the movie case and put it in the DVD player. He sat down as Bruce used the remote to push "play."

The movie started out spooky enough. It appeared to be some "summer camp" flick with hormone-driven teenagers chasing each other. The fun ended after the discovery of one teen's body in the forest, hacked to pieces.

"Gross!" Toby gasped.

"Awesome!" Bruce commented with wide eyes.

The movie intensified from there. The killer began hacking away at the campers with an axe. Gratuitous scenes of blood, body parts and chopped organs appeared. The boys recoiled as they watched.

"This is intense!" Toby commented.

During one scene, the killer was standing in the woods with his axe, looking around.

Then he seemed to look at the screen.

The two teens screamed as the killer suddenly began climbing through the TV.

"What the fuck!" Toby screamed.

"This isn't happening!" Bruce cried in terror.

The killer emerged from the TV set and stood in the room, flashing an evil grin at the two friends on the couch.

"Run!" Bruce screamed, jumping up to run out of the room.

He heard Toby's screams behind him and turned to see the killer hack his friend to pieces. Blood splattered all over him and the room.

Toby's screams died as his body crumbled to the floor.

"NO!" Bruce cried.

The killer now looked at him, gripping the axe.

Bruce turned to run to the door, seeing his mother standing in another room.

"Mom, run!" he yelled.

At the front door, his bloody hands slipped on the doorknob as he tried to open it. He heard his mother scream behind him and turned to see the killer striking her with his axe.

"No! Mom!"

The killer stood and ran towards Bruce with the bloody axe. Bruce screamed, frozen in terror.

Hell Hath No Fury

"I'm excited for tonight!"

Cheyenne smiled at her girlfriend. "Me, too. I have a feeling that we're going to win."

"We have to!" Her girlfriend insisted. "We've been working on these costumes all month! You are the spitten image of Gomez!"

"Thanks, Shelly. You are an amazing Morticia!"

They embraced and kissed.

"Will Dad be here soon?"

The couple parted and Cheyenne smiled at her 8-year-old son, wearing his cowboy costume. She looked at her watch and frowned. "He was supposed to be here an hour ago." She retrieved her cell phone from her pocket. "I'll call."

She smiled as she watched Shelly turn to leave the room with her son, then listened as the line rang.

It went to voicemail. After the recording, she said, "Hey, Shawn. Are still taking Ben trick-or-treating tonight? Give me a call. Bye."

Cheyenne walked out of the bedroom to find Ben and Shelly at the front door, handing out candy to trick-or-treaters. Once they closed the door and turned, Shelly looked at her with concern. "We're going to be late."

"We'll take him with us," she said.

"Really?" Ben exclaimed with excitement.

Cheyenne smiled at him. "Really."

To Shelly, she mouthed, "Sorry."

The costume party wasn't really meant for little kids, being held at the drag club. But Cheyenne tried to make the best of things, getting Ben excited over neat costumes on display and plying him with unlimited chicken wings.

After no answer trying to reach Shawn for the third time, Cheyenne tapped Shelly's arm. "I'm heading out for a smoke."

Shelly nodded and indicated she would stay with Ben.

Cheyenne made her way through the crowded club and headed out the entrance. Standing by her car in the parking lot, she lit her cigarette and took a long drag.

The nicotine did little to calm her rage.

She grabbed her cell phone with her free hand and was about to dial Shawn again when something caught her eye across the street.

"What the fuck?"

Across the street, Shawn had his arm around a woman she didn't know, leading her into a restaurant.

Growling, Cheyenne pocketed her phone and crushed her cigarette under her shoe. She stormed across the street and went into the restaurant. She found Shawn at a table with the woman, laughing at something.

"If he gets to ruin my night, I get to ruin his," she whispered to herself.

She made a quick phone call on her cell phone then put it away.

She glided over to his table, smiling.

"Hey, stranger, guess what?" she cheerfully greeted.

Shawn looked at her with surprise.

"Remember that story you told me? About that body you buried in the woods?"

His look turned to horror.

"Well, the police know all about it now," she continued. "And they're on their way."

"You bitch!" he roared, jumping to his feet with a knife he pulled from his inner coat pocket.

Cheyenne swung back, causing Shawn to stab a nearby waiter instead.

Her Deathversary

"Today is a special day," Lily signed to her sister. "It is Mother's deathversary."

Her sister's eyes widened. "Oh. I forgot," she signed in response.

Lily frowned. "We can't forget Mother, June," she signed. "We must follow the old ways, or she will be mad."

"But she is dead," June signed.

"Never anger the dead," Lily reminded in sign language.

June nodded in understanding. She had been taught this lesson many times before. Besides, Lily was older than her and knew the old ways better.

Lily's husband, Duncan, however, was not so agreeable.

"Get that shit off of my table!" he growled at Lily, pointing at the makeshift altar on the kitchen table.

Lily frowned at him then pointed at her deaf sister. "In sign language, please!" she signed to him as she spoke. "And I can't. It's Mother's deathversary. We must honor her at our kitchen table."

"This is ridiculous!" he complained, refusing to sign. "We're supposed to remember people when they're born, not when they die."

"Both passages through the world are important," Lily signed.

"Not in my house." He swiped the photo, food, burning candle and their mother's treasured necklace onto the floor. "Now clean that shit up!"

He stormed out of the room.

Lily felt shock and rage flood through her over the destruction of their beautiful altar constructed in their mother's memory. Then she noticed her sister looking at her with horror.

"Don't worry," she signed. "Mother will get him."

The sisters set up a new altar at the family hearth. They sat next to it holding hands. When the time of their mother's death rolled around, they began to reflect on memories they shared with her.

Screams from another area of the house brought Lily out of her thoughts. Upon realizing why they were happening, she ignored them. She knew it was only Mother having her revenge.

She smiled at June, blissfully unaware of what was happening. June smiled back.

She turned around and watched as her husband stumbled towards her. Upon noticing her sister's posture, June also turned to look at what her sister stared at.

The black ghost of their mother straddled Lily's husband's shoulders, her sharp nails clawed into his eyes. Blood dripped down his cheeks and mouth. Lily noticed a gaping hole in his chest, where his heart had been.

Their ghostly mother tore her fingers from the empty eye sockets and his body sunk to the floor. The ghost stood, smiling at her daughters. Then she faded away.

The sisters looked at each other.

"Even in death, Mother takes care of us," Lily signed.

June nodded in agreement.

Her Last Halloween

Carter had high hopes for his friend's Halloween party, but as time passed, he had to admit: Things were getting pretty boring.

He was about to get his jacket when something caught his eye on the way to the closet. In another room, where teenagers dressed in various Halloween costumes were dancing to music, he spotted a girl standing in the corner. She had long red hair and wore a fairy costume. She appeared to be his age, fifteen, but he couldn't remember seeing her anywhere.

She sadly looked out at the partygoers. Carter got the impression she wished she could join them.

He hadn't seen her all evening, and if he had, he would have at least introduced himself. She looked lonely.

He walked into the room and to where she stood. She smiled at him once she noticed him.

"Hi," he greeted.

"Hi," she replied, smiling. "What's your name?"

"Carter. What's yours?"

"My name is Elosia," she replied, her green eyes twinkling. "Nice to meet you, Carter."

"Nice to meet you, too."

They walked around the house, chatting. Carter ignored the strange looks he got from the partygoers.

At one point, Elosia turned to look at him. "I have to go home now." She sighed. "This is my last Halloween."

Carter studied her. "Why do you say that?"

She sadly shook her head. "I just know." She turned to walk to the front door, where someone had just opened it to a group of trick-or-treaters standing on the porch. Elosia walked around them as she left.

"Wait!" Carter called. He ran out the door, around the trick-or-treaters, to follow her. Once he caught up to her, she turned to look at him. "Let me walk you home."

She smiled. "Okay."

They talked a bit more as they walked. Carter began to feel uneasy as they entered the nearby woods. "This is how you get home?"

"it's a shortcut," Elosia replied.

Carter nervously looked around. At one point, he noticed Elosia was no longer at his side. "Elosia?" he called, looking around.

No answer.

He wandered until he found her, standing in the distance next to a tree with her back to him.

"Thought I lost you," he said, walking towards her.

Then he froze.

"No!" Elosia screamed. She tried to run but a man appeared and grabbed her. He shook her as he strangled her.

"Stop!" Carter yelled, running towards them.

They disappeared right when he got to the spot. Carter looked around in confusion. Then he looked down and saw Elosia's body on the ground. Gasping, he jumped back.

"I told you it was my last Halloween," a voice said at his side.

He looked up to see Elosia wearing the same costume as the body on the ground.

She looked at him and smiled. "Thank you for spending time with me tonight. It gets so lonely sometimes."

Carter watched in shock as Elosia walked off, eventually fading into the air among the trees.

I'll Be Dying Soon

"Thank you for visiting with me."

I smiled and nodded my response as I put the jacket on.

"It means a lot," my mother continued as I turned to leave. "Especially since I'll be dying soon."

I froze in my tracks. This was new. Was she trying to guilt-trip me for not visiting her so often?

I turned around. Knowing I would regret this, I asked, "Why do you say that?"

My mother shrugged like it wasn't such a big deal. "Because it's the truth. My time to go is near."

Sighing, I walked over to where she sat in her recliner. "Mother, please don't talk like that. Nobody knows when they are going to die."

"But I do!" she replied with enthusiasm, looking at me as though she now knew a special secret. "He told me last night. In my dream."

Now I was curious. Maybe this wasn't her guilt-tripping me after all. Maybe this was one of her delusions. Alzheimer's can do that sometimes.

"Who told you?" I finally asked.

"The Grim Reaper," she answered. She said it like she was talking about the weather. As though the Grim Reaper was in everybody's dreams lots of times.

"O-kay," I replied, choosing my words carefully. Then I smiled at her. "Well, the next time you see the Grim Reaper, give him my regards."

I turned to leave but froze.

The Grim Reaper stood not two feet from me. Seeing it with my own eyes was surreal. At first, I couldn't believe what I was seeing. No way was I seeing the actual Grim Reaper.

But every ounce of my being knew it was the real thing. This was really the Grim Reaper.

It moved past me, though I really don't know how. It....floated, I guess. I didn't hear footsteps.

Then it was at my mother's side. It looked down at her and she looked up at it. She smiled, as if this thing was an old friend.

It offered its free hand to her and she took it. Then she rose out of the chair and started to walk right past me with it.

The Grim Reaper stopped moving when it stood alongside me. It turned to look directly at me and a chill raced down my spine at the darkness within its hood. "Soon," it said.

Then they both were in front of me again. I watched in stunned silence as their images disappeared.

I turned and my heart sank at the sight of my mother's body slumped forward in her recliner. I didn't need to feel for a pulse to know she was dead. I just knew.

And, she had been right all along. What she had seen was real.

What I had seen was real.

I turned to leave the room, practically running through the care facility to get out of that place and get to my car. I had to hurry. I had a lot of things to do.

After all, I'll be dying soon.

Killer Toes

Rod plopped into the recliner and kicked off his shoes. His feet itched so he took off his socks to scratch them. Then he popped open a beer and took a long swig.

"Oh, that's gross!" his roommate commented.

Rod looked from the TV he was watching to his friend. "What?"

"Your toes, dude," his roommate replied, pointing at them. "They're all purple and disgusting."

Rod flipped up the footrest on the recliner and his legs straightened as it popped up. He examined his toes and chuckled. "Wow. That's awesome."

"No, it's not!" his roommate disagreed. "They're gross!"

Rod shrugged. "I stepped in some weird swamp shit at the job site today. I guess it seeped through my shoes. I'll take a shower later."

"Or you could take one now?" his roommate suggested. "They stink, too!"

"Later," Rod said, relaxing in the recliner as he watched TV.

His roommate fell silent as he remained on the couch, watching TV too. But soon Rod heard gagging sounds.

He looked at his roommate. "Bart, you ok?"

Bart appeared to be having a seizure. Then he gripped his throat and keeled over onto the floor.

Rod jumped from his seat to examine his friend. "Bart! Bart, are you okay?"

He felt for a pulse but there was none. His roommate was dead.

Days after Bart's funeral, and after having taken several showers, the purple coloring on Rod's toes was still there. They also still emitted a foul odor, which Rod confirmed from smelling them.

He sighed as he sat on the bottom of his bed one day, looking at his toes.

"Bart was right," he said. "They are gross."

An invisible cloud of smoke emitted from tiny holes the toxic sewage had created underneath his toenails.

The odorless smoke rose to his face and went into his nose. Rod's eyes widened as he asphyxiated and felt a tightening in his chest. His body shook as though he was having a seizure, the poison from the smoke racing through his body.

His heart exploded and his body fell back on his bed.

What was left of the smoke remaining in the air returned to filter into the holes on his toes.

Monday Coffee

Brian didn't send the text. He always sent the text, every Friday at noon.

Jonah started to worry. Was there gonna be a change of plans today? Did something come up? If they weren't going to meet for coffee today like they did every Monday after work, he didn't want to show up there and wait all day for him.

He went anyway. Brian was there, sitting at a table with his coffee. Jonah got in line to get his coffee then sat across from Brian at the table, smiling.

Brian didn't smile back.

When Brian finally looked at him, Jonah nodded. "What's up?"

Brian's hardened gaze bore into him. "Why'd ya do it?"

Jonah shook his head, looking at him with confusion. "Do what?"

"Hurt that kid."

Jonah looked around, appearing uneasy. Once he made sure that no one was paying attention to them, he leaned across the table. "Let's not talk about that here."

"Well, we're talking about it," Brian said, scowling. He pointed a finger at Brian as he spoke. "He was just a kid."

Jonah hardened his gaze. "He ignored the rules."

Brian scoffed. "Come on! You put out a bowl of candy, telling the trick-or-treaters to only take one, what do you think was going to happen?"

Jonah shrugged. "That they would only take one."

"That's bullshit, and you know it."

Jonah shook his head in disagreement, relaxing in his chair. "Kids gotta learn to obey the rules."

"But we shouldn't hurt them if we don't," Brian pointed out. "You chased after that kid and shook him pretty damn hard. He pissed his pants! You're lucky there weren't any adults around."

Jonah stood from the table, holding his coffee. "Deal with it, Brian. There's no shame in my game."

Brian jumped to his feet, knocking the chair over behind him. "I'm not gonna deal with it, because that was my kid!"

Jonah's look of surprise turned to alarm as Brian swung his fist through the air, hitting his friend in the left jaw. Jonah flew backwards onto the ground, his coffee flying from his hand.

Brian stood over him. "Next time, pick on someone your own size! And do me a favor: Lose my number."

Then he stormed off.

No Rest For the Wicked

Reneta closed her eyes, her tired body relaxing in bed.

"Get up, lazy girl!" a woman's voice shrieked. "There is cleaning to do!"

Reneta groaned. "Go away, Mom."

She yelped when the ghostly image of her mother, dead for six years, appeared in front of her. Despite the darkness of her bedroom, she could clearly see the face.

"There is laundry to be folded!" her mother shrieked. "And dirty dishes in the sink!"

"I'll do that tomorrow," Reneta said

Her mother yanked the blanket away. "You'll do it NOW! Get up!"

Groaning in exhaustion, Reneta sat up in bed and switched on the lamp on her bedside table. She rubbed the sleep from her eyes and stood. Her mother's ghost followed right behind her as she left her bedroom.

"I thought you were going to bed?" her roommate asked as she passed Reneta in the hallway.

"No rest for the wicked," Reneta muttered, as she had so many times before.

So Reneta removed her clothes from the dryer and folded them before putting them away. Then she washed the three dirty dishes in the sink.

She started walking back to her room, yawning.

"Where are you going?" her mother shouted.

Reneta froze, her spine tingling at the icy presence of her mother's ghost right behind her.

"There is dust on your bookcases!" her mother shouted. "Get rid of it!"

Sighing, she turned and walked to the kitchen cabinet where they kept the cleaning supplies. She opened it and removed the duster. She walked over to one of the two bookcases in the living room and removed the two picture frames on top of it before dusting.

Finished, she put the duster back.

"Those windows are filthy!" her mother's ghost shouted behind her. "Clean them!"

Reneta quietly obeyed. After cleaning all of the windows in her apartment, she once again felt her mother's ghost right behind her.

"Vacuum that carpet!" her mother's ghost ordered. "It's dirty."

Reneta vacuumed the living room carpet, moving chairs and plants where needed.

Once she finished the vacuuming, she returned the vacuum cleaner to the cabinet. Then she turned to face her mother's ghost.

The angry scowl on the ghost's face was gone, replaced by a satisfied smile. "Good girl," it said. "Now go to bed."

"Thank you, Mother," Reneta replied.

As she climbed into bed, Reneta sighed with gratitude that now, finally, at last she could rest.

This was her life ever since her mother died and she was used to it.

One day, Reneta fell ill and had to be rushed to the hospital. The doctor gave her medication and ordered her to rest.

But after she got home, her ghostly mother would not let her rest.

"No rest for the wicked!" she screeched. "Get up and mop the floors!"

Reneta obeyed, as she always did. But when her lifeless body fell to the wet floor, her mother's ghost stood over her, yelling at her to get back up.

Perfect Decorations

Mary smiled as she examined her work. "It's perfect!"

Cloth ghosts hung from corners in the room. A garland of tiny jack-o-lanterns ran along the wall. A string of lights with tiny lit ghosts along the cord hung beneath the window sill. Various Halloween decorations hung along the walls and electric Halloween candles in the shapes of ghosts, monsters and jack-o-lanterns decorated the coffee table.

"Pathetic!" a voice growled behind her.

Mary rolled her eyes as she turned to face what she knew was the ghost that had been haunting her apartment the entire month she'd lived there. This time, when she turned to look at it, it was fully visible. Just as she imagined, the voice belonged to the ghost of an elderly man. He had white hair, wrinkles on his face and aged, knotted hands that appeared from the sleeves of his red sweater. He also wore black pants and brown loafers.

She folded her arms across her chest. "I suppose you have a better idea for Halloween decorations?"

"You're darn tootin' I do!" he replied, shaking his finger at her. He looked around. "We never had these flimsy, miserable excuses of decorations for All Hallows! Back in my day, we really knew how to celebrate the occasion! Things like straw men on the doors, bobbing for apples, and *real* candles! Not those fake electric things."

Mary shook her head. "Those 'fake electric things' are safer and last longer. The last thing I want to do is burn my apartment down."

"In my day, we knew how to be careful with candles!" the ghost replied with an air of indignation.

"Well, this isn't your day, or your apartment, either." She turned away, smiling as she walked to the kitchen. "It's mine, and I get to decorate it any way I want to."

A pounding at her door stopped her in her tracks. She hurried over to it. "Who's there?" she called.

No answer. She looked through the peephole but didn't see anything.

She unlocked her door and opened it. Before she could step over the threshold, a man grabbed her neck and pushed her inside the apartment, closing the door behind him.

"You bitch!" he roared. "You and your fucking text! You're never getting rid of me!"

Mary struggled to get free from his grip on her neck but it was too tight. She coughed as she trued to breathe.

"Hey, creep!"

He turned his head to look and the next thing Mary saw was blood flying everywhere.

She stood in shock, slowly removing the hand still gripped around her neck. She looked down to see it was without an arm and shrieked as she dropped it.

Then she looked around.

Her now ex- and late boyfriend's blood was all ovcer her walls. Body parts lay scattered on the floor.

The ghost appeared at her side as she examined the new decoration. "Not bad," he said.

"It's pretty good," she agreed, nodding. She smiled at the ghost. "Thanks."

Routines

Insomnia has me mindlessly wandering around my apartment. No, I wasn't seeing a doctor about it. Yes, I had it under control. Well, more or less. It was just something I had to deal with.

The usual routines were performed: I played video games, cooked some food, watched TV, read a book and stood at the living room window, just staring outside. There were hardly any people out on the street in my neighborhood at this time. It was 3:00 in the morning. Normal people were sleeping. I wondered what it was like to be able to just fall asleep at night and not wake up until morning. Haven't done that for a long time.

A knock at my door surprised me. Who on earth would be knocking at my door at this hour? A fellow insomniac looking for company?

I walked over to the door and looked out the peephole. It's my friend Chris, in his pizza uniform. Ah, yes. Someone else with a sleep disorder. Chris sleepwalks. But he doesn't just walk, though. He has been known to do things in his sleepwalking adventures, like work on his car, buy a sack of sugar from the store or take the bus across town. Amazingly, he has never been hurt!

They say never to awaken someone who is sleepwalking and nobody has ever tried when Chris goes on one of his nocturnal escapades. Up until now, it was all harmless stuff, so nobody bothered him. The fact that he was actually able to do things while sleepwalking is amazing in itself!

I opened the door and sighed. So now he was performing his job: Delivering a pizza. This was definitely one for the books.

"Chris, it's 3AM," I said. "We don't order or deliver pizza at 3AM. Go home."

His eyes remained glazed and his face emotionless. "Pizza delivery," he said, shoving the box at me. Then he turned to leave.

I shake my head, clutching the box as I turn and close the door. I locked the door and turned to walk to the kitchen. I had already had something to eat, so I really wasn't in the mood for pizza. But I was curious what kind of pizza it was.

I opened the pizza box and gasped.

Apparently, Chris was up to his old routines again. That's how I came to meet him, you see. Both of us are ex-cons, guilty of murder.

Except now, with his sleepwalking, Chris was reverting back to an old routine of his from his killing days.

There in the pizza box lay the beating heart of his newest victim.

Something There

Josie and David, both twenty, hid behind bushes as they looked at the towering house across the street.

"Are you sure it's haunted?" she asked.

"Of course I'm sure," David replied. "You watched that episode of *Ghost Freaks* too. They clearly said this house had ghosts."

"They also said it was abandoned," Josie pointed out. "But there are lights on inside."

David nodded. "Maybe it's on a timer."

"Or maybe somebody lives there?" Josie asked, looking at him. "Last time I checked, trespassing is illegal."

David squeezed his girlfriend's hand. "Hey, do you want to see a ghost or not?"

She smiled. "Let's go ghosting."

They emerged from their hiding spot and scoured the area as they moved closer to the house. They checked for a darkened window to climb through or an open cellar door.

Just when the two of them got to the backyard, Josie gripped David's arm. "David! I saw someone!"

"Where?" he asked, looking at the house towering above them.

Josie pointed to a window. "There. I saw someone looking out." She shot him a nervous look. "Maybe they saw us?"

"If they did, they didn't do anything," her boyfriend replied, waving it off. "Come on. Let's try this window."

They crept towards a nearby window of a darkened room. David reached up to grip the bottom frame of the window when a loud *THUMP!* Met their ears. He froze. "What was that?"

"I don't know!" Josie whispered in response. "I think there's something there."

His fear gone, David shrugged. "Maybe it was a cat." He proceeded to grab the frame. Surprisingly, the window slid open. He smiled at Josie. "Let's go."

They climbed through the window into the dark room. But before they could begin exploring, the door to the room slowly creaked open, revealing light from the hallway.

"Is it a ghost?" Josie asked in a surprised whisper.

"Just the door," David replied. "Shh! Be careful."

They crept through the room and David carefully scanned the hallway. Indicating it was safe, he led Josie out into the hallway. They kept an eye out for anyone as they walked to the end.

"The ghost is supposed to be in the library," David whispered.

They exited the hallway, entering a dark room that appeared to be the lobby. They carefully moved on to another dark room, finally noticing a nearby door ajar to a lit room.

"I think that's the library," David whispered. "Come on."

They used the faint light in the room to creep towards the door. Just before they reached it, a sound of rattling chains hit their ears and they froze.

"David, I'm scared!" Josie whispered.

"It's okay," David assured.

They crept to the door and it creaked as it opened.

A man jumped in front of them. "Boo!"

The couple screamed then turned to run to the front door. The man's laughter echoed behind them as they ran out of the house and as far away as they could get.

Spaghetti Face

Rhea studied the man who just sat down at the table across from her. He had been wearing a paper bag over his head in his profile picture and here he was on their date, still wearing the bag.

"Hi, I'm Jeff," he greeted.

She brushed aside the chill racing down her spine, ignoring the strange looks from the people in the diner. She forced a smile. "Hi, Jeff. I didn't realize you wore that thing in public."

He shrugged. "I wore it in my profile picture."

"I thought it was a joke."

"It's no joke," he replied. "I have to wear it."

She nodded. "Okay." She nervously stirred the spoon in her coffee, which was probably cold by now. She removed the spoon and placed it on the table before looking at him again. "Why do you wear it?"

"Because people won't like my real face," he answered.

She swallowed the lump in her throat. The poor man. Her revulsion turned to sympathy as she reached out across the table to squeeze his hand. "I'm sure your face is fine."

"It's not," he replied.

She smiled.

After leaving the diner, they decided to walk around the neighborhood. They chatted and asked each other the usual getting-to-know-you questions.

Their stroll eventually led them to a cemetery.

Jeff stopped at the entrance gate and stared at the graves. "I like coming here."

Rhea felt a tingle of excitement. "Really? Me, too."

He turned his head to look at her. "Let's go inside."

He opened the gate and they walked along the cement path leading into the cemetery. Rhea looked at a tombstone every now and then.

Jeff came to a stop in front of one of the graves. She stood at his side, reading the tombstone. "Madigan Percel, March 19, 1872-August 23, 2023, Town Mage."

Rhea studied those last two words. She looked at Jeff. "Town mage?"

Jeff nodded. "He was a wizard." He looked at her. "He's the one who gave me my face."

Rhea stifled the urge to laugh. Did this guy have a Harry Potter fixation, or something? Was there a lightning bolt scar on his forehead?

"It can't be that bad," she decided to say instead.

"It is," Jeff replied. "He knew how much I loved spaghetti, so he made me have spaghetti for the rest of my life."

Curious now, Rhea stood in front of him. She removed the bag from his head then stifled a scream. Jeff's entire face was a mix of spaghetti. His nose was even a meatball.

"He says he wants to give you spaghetti for the rest of your life, too," Jeff said now.

Bile raced up her throat and Rhea ran out of the cemetery. Just as she passed through the gate, her face suddenly felt strange. She noticed she was dripping a red sauce to the ground.

She raised her hands to her face and screamed in horror once she felt the stringy saucy pasta surrounding her entire face.

Spooky Season

"It's not Halloween yet!"

Susan ignored her husband's remark. "It's not Halloween," she answered. "But it *is* spooky season." She smiled at him and held out her arms. "Wanna help me decorate?"

"No, thanks," he muttered. "It's stupid! I wish you never decorated for Halloween." He stormed out of the room.

Susan placed her hands on her hips. "You never want to help."

"I can help," a voice spoke from behind her.

Susan turned to see a young boy of about ten years old.

"Well," she greeted, walking over to him. She smiled as she placed her hands on her knees and looked in his brown eyes. "Look who's here."

"Yes, I'm here," he replied, nodding.

"You were hiding, weren't you?" she asked.

He nodded again.

She straightened. "It's about time we get a proper introduction." She held out her hand. "My name is Susan. What about you?"

"I'm Ryan," he answered, smiling up at her as he shook her hand.

Susan nodded. "Okay, Ryan. If you're going to help me decorate for Halloween, we better get started."

The boy followed her to the large orange bin containing various Halloween decorations she had placed on the floor of the living room.

The two of them chatted on various topics as they worked, laughing at jokes and sharing stories of old Halloween adventures.

Once she'd hung the last decoration on the wall, which was a paper skull with pumpkins all around the side, she slapped her hands together with satisfaction.

"Okay, Ryan, that's it!" she announced, turning to face the room.

Ryan smiled at her.

"I can't believe this!" Susan's husband complained, storming into the room. He examined the decorations and shook his head in disgust. "For fuck's sake, it's only August! Take this shit back down!"

Susan stared at him with shock. "I will not! You know how much I love Halloween!"

"Yeah, well, I don't!" he yelled. "And since I make more money than you do, I'm the boss around here! Take this stuff down now, or I'll throw it all away!"

Susan took a step forward. "You wouldn't!"

He nodded. "Oh, I will. Watch me!"

He walked over to yank a paper decoration of a ghost off of the wall and began tearing it up.

"No! Don't!" Susan pleaded, running over to him to stop him.

"Shut up!" he roared, slapping her on the face.

Susan flew to the floor.

"Ghosts are stupid!" he exclaimed.

"No, we're not," a voice said.

He turned and dropped the remains of the decoration to the floor as he seized up in pain. He grabbed his chest and cried out in agony. Then his body fell to the floor.

Ryan stood over him, smiling.

Susan slowly got to her feet, looking at her dead husband. She felt the sensitive spot on her face where he had hit her. It hadn't been the first time.

"Are you okay?" Ryan asked, looking at her.

She smiled at him. "I am now."

Sweet Revenge

Angus froze. Right at the next house stood Barry and Sampson, the two bullies from his school. They were dressed up like bikers and right when they turned away from the door they had trick-or-treated at, he could see the devilish looks on their faces.

They were up to no good, like always.

Angus hid behind a nearby bush as he watched the boys step onto the sidewalk and proceed down the street. They chatted, oblivious to the people around them.

Angus carefully followed behind them, no longer caring about trick-or-treating.

At some point, the bullies stole the bag of candy from a girl dressed as a ballerina and pushed her onto somebody's yard. Then they ran off, laughing.

Angus shook his head in disgust. Even when they weren't at school, the bullies still acted like bullies.

He ran ahead to catch up to them. He found them hanging out in front of a house. He took a candy bar from his bag of candy, opened the top of it, and removed a sharp rock from his pocket. He pushed the rock into the back of the candy bar.

He made sure he was standing close enough where the bullies could hear him then took a tiny bite off of the top of the candy bar.

"This candy is so good!" he exclaimed.

"Let me be the judge of that!" Barry said, grabbing the candy and pushing him away. He took a large bite of the candy bar and started chewing it.

Then he dropped his bags of candy as he started coughing.

Angus smiled as he bent over to pick up the girl's stolen bag of candy. Then he turned and walked back to where he had last seen her, enjoying the sounds of Barry choking on the rock.

Teacher Problems

"Don't go to Open House, Mom. It's stupid!"

Sandy ignored her son's whining. "I don't think it's stupid. Besides, I need to go. I have to schedule a conference with your teacher."

Her son frowned. "My teachers aren't very nice."

"You say that about all of your teachers," she joked, tousling her 9-year-old's hair.

"But this time, I mean it!" he said. "Don't go, Mom. Please."

"Don't worry," she said, walking past him.

Once things were settled with the babysitter, Sandy left. At the Open House at her son's elementary school, she enjoyed touring the classrooms, admiring photos and looking at a variety of school assignments and projects her son had completed.

"Your Andy's mom?"

She looked up at the gentleman who appeared by her son's desk, which she had just finished looking at the papers on it. She smiled, immediately feeling a sense of attraction to him.

"Yes, my name is Sandy Harper," she answered, extending her hand for him to shake.

"Pleased to meet you, I'm Tom Blakely," he replied, shaking her hand. "Andy is a delight to have in my classroom. He's so smart and so creative!"

Sandy's grin broadened. "Thank you. I never knew he took such a strong interest in math."

Tom nodded. "He always comes up with interesting ways to solve problems. He even helps out some of his peers."

They continued talking, and the more that Sandy got to know this teacher, the more she wondered why her son didn't like him. Then she noticed that he had sharp incisor teeth at the edges of his upper teeth. A chill ran down her spine. They looked like vampire teeth!

She shook her head. Perhaps she was just imagining things.

She had that same thought again when she met Andy's P.E. coach, who she noticed had only one eye. The art teacher spoke in poems, urging the children to create things and ending her poems with "So mote it be!" And the science teacher kept having either his arm fall off of his body or his head began to slide off the neck before he quickly adjusted it.

As Sandy walked to the final classroom on the tour, where her son attended his English and Reading studies, she noticed the blinds in the room covered all the windows. This teacher appeared normal, a man in his thirties with brown hair dressed in brown pants and a white buttoned shirt.

This teacher, Mr. Blaine Hanson, smiled at Sandy as he greeted her. The conversation went well until he noticed a child opening the blind.

"No, stop!" he cried.

The blind went up and the full moon shone through the window. Sandy gasped as she watched Blaine transform into a werewolf. He roared with hunger. Everyone in the room screamed as they ran out of the classroom. Sandy turned to run but felt a claw grab the color of her blouse and yank her back. She screamed as sharp teeth bit into her shoulder.

The Dream That Never Ends

"You need to let me go." She huddled in the dark area of the room, wrapping her arms around the knees she bent against her chest. She stared up at the portrait, but the only sign the man had heard her was a smile slowly forming on his face.

A tear ran down her cheek and she wiped it away. "Please. I want to wake up now. I want to get back to my life."

Nothing happened then. She bent her head onto her knees and sobbed, finally releasing the pain welling in her chest.

"This is your home now."

She gasped, standing as she looked at the portrait. The man was no longer in it. She looked around the area of the room where the light shone over the portrait but didn't see him.

"And you will never wake up again."

She knew where he was now. She turned to face him, hardening her gaze. "I'm not afraid of you."

The man that was one moment ago dressed as a bullfighter shifted as he stepped closer. She gulped in terror as he transformed into Satan. "You should be."

She turned and ran, his laughter echoing behind her. "Wake up! Wake up!" she screamed, hoping her sleeping self would somehow hear her. "Come on, Amber! Wake up!"

She continued to run through the tunnel, this time thankful that there was nothing in it.

The man appeared in front of her and she gasped as she ran into him. Her body flew backwards onto the floor, and suddenly the dark tunnel around them was one. Now they were in a large room with a crystal chandelier hanging above them. Music played in the background and the sounds of voices appeared.

The man was now dressed in a tuxedo. He reached out to her. "Shall we dance?"

Amber looked down to see that instead of the blue jeans and red T-shirt she had worn moments ago, she was now wearing a wedding dress. Before she could say anything, a force swept her up onto her feet and she flew into the man's arms.

She gasped as he held her close and began dancing with her. They danced for hours and she thought they would never stop.

Then when he tired of the dancing, they entertained themselves at a cinema, watching the ballet. Then He arranged the dream to where they sailed the vast oceans on the yacht.

She considered herself lucky that at least now the dream was pleasant. She knew to never again plead to him to let her awaken from the dream – otherwise, he would torture her again. He'd use a whip on her, slice her limbs off or lock her naked body up inside of a small crate, where she was tortured for hours with the heat.

As long as she kept him in a good mood and did his bidding, the dream was at least pleasant. A dream from which she now knew she would never awaken from.

The Scary Costume

Waylon opened the door and gasped. His blood chilled and his heart froze in terror. Standing on the porch was the scariest costume he had seen all night. This particular costume consisted of the person wearing a black cloak, a menacing pumpkin mask, and holding a large battle axe in one hand.

"Trick or treat!" the person wearing the costume said, holding out a bag. The bag already had a large amount of candy in it.

Waylon swallowed the lump of fear in his throat. It's just a costume, he told himself. He had to prove to his parents that, at seven years old, he was indeed old enough to answer the door for trick or treaters.

He took a step closer, clutching the big orange plastic bowl of candy in his arms. He strengthened his grip of the bowl with one arm as he reached in to grab one of the small candies and put it into the person's bag.

"Thanks," they said, nodding.

They turned to walk away.

"Happy Halloween!" Waylon called, wondering if they heard him.

He watched as the person eventually disappeared from view then shuddered as he moved back to close the door. Once he was safely against the closed door, he sighed. "That costume was scary!"

He hoped that was the end of that, but after he fell asleep that night, that costumed person was in his dream, chasing him through the wood. Waylon screamed as he ran.

He still screamed as he awoke from the nightmare. His parents ran into the room to comfort him, assuring him that it was only a dream.

Waylon believed that line of reasoning at first — until he had that nightmare again the next evening. After the fourth night of having that nightmare, his parents took him to a doctor.

"It's just a phase," the doctor told them. "He'll stop having the nightmares at some point."

"But I never did," twenty-year-old Waylon explained to the psychiatrist now. "And tomorrow I turn twenty-one. That's fourteen years of the same nightmare!"

The psychiatrist shook her head. "Waylon, that's not possible." She sighed. "I can increase your dosage, as requested. If it will help you."

Waylon nodded. He didn't expect her to believe him. None of the shrinks he'd been to ever did. "Thank you," he mumbled.

The guard escorted Waylon back to his jail cell. As Waylon lay on his bunk that night, trying to forget the screams of the women he had murdered, he prepared himself for the same nightmare.

It happened as predicted: The pumpkinhead monster chased him through the woods. Waylon screamed, running. Unlike the many other dreams, this time he tripped and fell to the ground.

He flipped over and gasped in terror as the monster drew closer, raising its axe for the kill.

"This isn't supposed to happen!" Waylon cried. He screamed as the axe came swinging down on his head.

What remained of his body was found in the jail cell the next morning.

The Secret Ingredient

Margaret entered the kitchen and smiled at the sight of her niece mixing ingredients in a bowl. A cookbook lay open on the counter nearby. She walked over to read the page. "You're making the pie!" she said, looking at her teenaged niece.

Her niece smiled at her. "I just *love* pumpkin pie and wanted to try it."

Margaret nodded in agreement, her eyes moving across the used ingredients along the counter. Then she frowned. "Ye gods, Katrina. Canned pumpkin?" she asked with surprise, looking at her niece again.

Katrina shrugged with embarrassment. "I know the recipe says to use the pumpkin from a fresh pumpkin, but canned pumpkin is basically the same thing."

Margaret sighed as she closed her eyes. How sad that the new generation continued to ignore the old ways. Fresh pumpkin was what always made the pie stand out.

Still, Katrina had a point. As long as she used the more important ingredients, that was all that mattered.

"If you say so, dear," she mumbled, walking to the refrigerator. "Is your mother still out shopping?"

"Yes, she said she'll be back soon," Katrina replied. "She's having trouble finding an herb."

Margaret nodded as she removed a jug of orange juice from the refrigerator. "Probably the burdock root. It's so hard to find these days."

"I'm sure she'll find it," Katrina replied. "I cast a good luck spell for her."

Margaret smiled as she poured her juice. "Good girl."

She put the jug of orange juice away and walked back to the counter. Before she could take a sip from her glass, she noticed her niece looking at her.

"What's this?" Katrina asked, pointing at something on the opened cookbook.

Margaret walked over to read what she pointed at then smiled. "It means blood of kin."

Katrina blinked. "Blood?" Then she made a disgusted look. "In pumpkin pie?"

Margaret shrugged, opening a drawer. "Oh, it's just a drop. Nobody will notice." She removed a chef's knife, checked the blade to ensure it was indeed sharpened, then proceeded to choose an area of her hand to cut.

"Wait, why not me?" Katrina asked.

"My dear, your magic is not strong enough for this," Margaret replied, looking at her. "You aren't even sixteen."

"My magic is just as good as yours," Katrina declared.

Margaret shrugged. "If you say so." She walked over to her niece, who smiled with excitement as she held her hand over the bowl of mixed ingredients. Margaret made a small nick in the girl's pointing finger, the magic finger, ignoring the girl's gasp as she watched the blood drop into the mix.

"There!" she announced, smiling as she turned to carry the knife to the sink and wash it off.

Just before they ate the pie for dessert that night, Katrina announced, "I added the secret ingredient!"

The women smiled then took a bite. Then they exploded.

Katrina sighed then shook her head. "I guess my magic was too strong."

The Sign

"FREE VACATION WITH ANY PURCHASE!"

Calvin stopped walking and stared at the sign. He noticed that his coworker had continued on and turned to look his way. "Hey, Raul! What do you think of this sign?" he called.

Raul turned in surprise then turned to walk back to where Calvin stood. He looked at the store window Calvin pointed at then back at him. "What sign?"

"There's a sign right there," Calvin replied, studying him. "Don't you see it?"

Raul looked at the store window again then back at him and shook his head. "I don't see it."

Calvin hardened his gaze as he looked at him. "How can you not see it? It's right there! With big letters on it!"

Raul studied the store window then looked at Calvin with concern. "Well, I don't see it."

"Well, *I* see it, and I'm going inside to get my free vacation!" Calvin shot back at him. Then he shook his head in exhaustion. "I could sure use one."

Raul smiled at him. "Whatever you say. Have fun. I'll catch you back at the office."

He turned and walked off.

Calvin walked into the store with determination, hoping there was something in there he could actually afford.

As luck would have it, he found a male grooming kit for only five dollars.

He hurried to the register and smiled at the cashier. "Hi! I'd like to buy this."

The cashier appeared to be an elderly man with black hair and black beady eyes. He wore a red shirt and red pants. He smiled at Calvin, who shuddered when he noticed the man's very sharp teeth. The man seemed to have two pointy things on either side of his head. He wore a name badge that read "STAN."

"Excellent choice, sir," the cashier said. "And with your purchase, you win a free vacation!"

"Great!" Calvin exclaimed, smiling as he pictured relaxing on a sandy beach with a nice cold drink in his hand. He removed his wallet from his rear pants pocket and took a five-dollar bill from inside it. He placed it on the counter and Stan picked it up to enter his purchase into the electronic cash register.

Once the five-dollar bill was placed into the cash drawer and the drawer was closed, Calvin smiled at Stan. "Where will I be going? Hawaii? The Bahamas?"

Stan chuckled. "Not quite." Then his eyes took on a fiery glow as he added, "You just won a vacation....to Hell!"

He pressed a button on the counter and a trapdoor opened beneath Calvin's feet.

Calvin screamed as he descended through blackness to a fiery pit below, the sound of Stan's laughter sounding from above him.

What We Do in the Dark

Zabien laughed with his friends as they walked along the street. At the end of the street was house that towered three stories high.

He looked at the house and sighed. "We can't go there," he said. He gestured to the front porch. "No lights on."

"Who cares?" the one standing closest to him, Jonah, dressed up as the clown from the movie *It*, said. "It's the last house on the street."

He turned and Zabien shrugged before he followed. Who knows? Maybe someone would answer. And maybe they handed out the good stuff: The king size candy bars.

He followed his friends up to the porch and waited as the one closest to the door knocked.

To their surprise, the door opened. The house inside was dark as well, but in the dimness of a small white light that came from a nightlight plugged into the wall, they could make out the shape of an elderly man.

"Trick or treat," they all chimed.

It was too dark to see the man's face, so none of them could tell if he was looking at any one of them in particular.

"Why is your house so dark?" Simon, dressed as a zombie, asked.

"We have to keep it dark," he replied. "We get headaches." He took a step forward and the group of friends took a step back. "And nobody can ever complain about what we do in the dark."

"What *do* you do in the dark?" Zabien asked.

The man was silent a moment and Zabien could almost feel the man's eyes on him. "We read," he finally answered.

Simon laughed but the others remained silent.

"I suppose you want your candy," he said now. "Here." He turned away from them to reach for something behind him then turned back around holding a large bowl. "Take your pick."

Because it was so dark, they couldn't see what kind of candy was in the bowl. They made do with grabbing whatever they could and moving away. "Thanks," Zabien said, before turning away.

The man grabbed Zabien's arm before he could turn away. "You're safer in the dark," he whispered.

Zabien nodded as if he understood some kind of secret, then turned away to walk off.

After he ate the candy at home, he groaned as a headache struck. It seemed to pound into his brain. As he struggled to get some pain relief medicine from the bathroom cabinet, he cried out in alarm when he realized there were tall, black figures all around him.

He turned off the light and they disappeared. His headache immediately went away.

He kept the lights off as he called his friends. "I had that happen, too," Jonah said. "I bet it was from the candy at that dark house," Simon threw in.

Zabien agreed. And to stay headache-free, as well as safe from the shadowy figures, the three of them spent the rest of their lives either wearing sunglasses or in a darkened room.

About the Author

Dawn Colclasure started writing at a young age and ever since has a collection of hundreds of poems, songs, essays, articles and short stories. She founded a poetry club, Circle of Poets, while in her teens, where she also edited and published their quarterly magazine, *American Bard*. She has had poetry and short stories published in anthologies and various magazines. She entered the professional writing world while in college, writing for her local newspaper while also working in the college newspaper department, then taking on a writing gig for a weekly webzine. From there she wrote her novel, *November's Child*, which was later published as *Shadow of Samhain*. She has also worked as a freelance writer, writing for magazines as well as E-zines. She worked as a poetry editor for Skyline E-Magazine. She began writing about deaf-related issues for the newspaper SIGNews, a national newspaper for the Deaf/HOH community. Because of her many ghostly sightings and paranormal experiences, she wanted to explore the paranormal in her writing, so she joined the team of writers for the Shadowlands site, writing about ghosts and hauntings. Writing a series of interviews for the website Write From Home inspired her to put together interviews for her book, *BURNING THE MIDNIGHT OIL: How We Survive as Writing Parents*, published in 2004. That same year, her second nonfiction book arrived: *365 Tips For Writers: Inspiration, Writing Prompts and Beat The Block Tips to Turbo Charge Your Creativity*. She has been writing various types of books ever since and to date has over four dozen books/ebooks published. After a negative experience with an independent publisher, who she worked for as an editor and marketing rep, she started self-publishing her poetry books, as well as her children's books. She continues to self-publish a variety of other books, mostly free ebooks for her newsletter. While being profoundly deaf as well as a burn survivor (the result of a vehicular accident when she was 20 months old), she has found that these challenges have helped her to work harder for success in her writing career and find new ways to work around communication challenges. These days, she publishes the SPARREW Newsletter, a monthly newsletter for self-publishers, authors, readers, reviewers, editors and writers. She works as a book reviewer and freelance writer while she continues writing a variety of books and ebooks. She lives with her husband and children in Oregon. In her spare time, she enjoys reading a variety of books as well as cooking, playing board games and going for walks. She is passionate about advocating for the rights of members of the LGBTQA+ community, the disabled community, as well as for women's rights. Her writing blog is at Dawn Colclasure's Blog[1]. You can find her on the Web at: https://dawnsbooks.com/ and https://www.dmcwriter.com/ Her Twitters: @dawnwilson325 and @dawncolclasure

---

1. http://dawncolclasureblog.blogspot.com/

Books by Dawn Colclasure

CHILDREN'S BOOKS:

The Yellow Rose
A Million Doughnuts
Hunter's Upcycling Adventures
Wolf Whispers
God's Birds
The Dream Forest

NONFICTION:

On the Wings of Pink Angels: Triumph, Struggle and Courage Against Breast Cancer
Terror In The Night I - Alien Abduction Exposed! (with Martha Jette and Usko Ahonen)
The Warrior Way
Parenting Pauses: Life as a Deaf Parent
A Ghost on Every Corner
Fabulously Frugal: How to Manage Your Money, Live for Less and Build Up Your Savings
Self-Care Suggestions Book
True Ghost Stories
The Idea Workbook: How to Choose and Use Your Ideas
10 Ways to Boost Your Mental Health

NOVELS:

Shadow of Samhain
Faded Reflection
Imprint
Lost Soul

POETRY:

Love is Like a Rainbow: Poems of Love and Devotion
Songs of the Dead
DOGS FOREVER: Poems for the Dog Person (with Jennifer Wilson)
Follow That Dream
Satyrs Are Cool: Poems of Mythological Creatures (with Jennifer Wilson)
Touched by Fire
April Showers
Remember the Soldier
Yesterday's Words
Wandering Soul
Seasonal Songs
Poems for the Grieving Heart
Ramblings & Misgivings
Dream World
We Will Never Have Enough Days
Savage World
Meditating Heart
The Power of Words
Tarnished Heart
A Tiny Light
The House That Madness Built

SHORT FICTION:

The Perfect Christmas
Remembering Sunny
5 Tales

WRITING:

BURNING THE MIDNIGHT OIL: How We Survive as Writing Parents
365 TIPS FOR WRITERS: Inspiration, Writing Prompts and Beat the Block
Tips to Turbo Charge Your Creativity

Burning the Midnight Oil Revisited
101 Quotes on Poetry
The Big Book of Writing Challenges
Free Stuff For Writers
Write for Your Life! The Health Benefits of Writing
The Newbie Author's Guide to Getting Your Book Published
Write Like the Wind! Inspirational Notes for Writers
Promote Your Book on a Shoestring...or Less

YOUNG READERS:

The GHOST Group, Book One (The Ghosts of Sarah Travers and The Crying Valentine)

The GHOST Group Book Two (The Ghost of the Irish Setter and The Ghost of the Missing Hiker)

The GHOST Group: Book Three (The Ghost of Calliope the Cat and The Fiery Viking)